Published by Three Muses Ink.

www.3musesink.com
Nisse at Night is a work of fiction. Names, characters, places, and incidents either are the product of the author's imagination or are used fictitiously, and any resemblance to actual persons, living or dead, business establishments, events or locales is entirely coincidental. The publisher does not have any control over and does not assume any responsibility for author or third-party websites or their content.

Kari L. Ronning
Nisse at Night

Nisse at Night©2014 Kari Ronning

Cover art, images, art, and graphics are by Kari Ronning©2014, Kari Ronning.

Edited by Daniel Wilson (MrProofReading) https://www.fiverr.com/mrproofreading

For rights information please email: **manager@3musesink.com**

ISBN 10: 0-988298-94-5
ISBN 13: 978-0-9882989-4-1

Library of Congress Control Number: 2016956240

Three Muses Ink presents
Storybook series

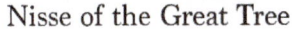

Nisse of the Great Tree

Mers in the Mist:
Scandinavian Water Myths

Mischief and Might:
The Monkey King

www.3MusesInk.com

For my Father

Nisse at Night:

Written and Illustrated
by Kari L. Ronning

www.3MusesInk.com

At night, when people are asleep, tucked tight in their warm blankets, covers heavy and snug… When the kitchen stands empty, all dishes washed and stored away, pots and pans hanging and hiding in cupboards…

When the moon climbs the rich velvet sky and the stars hum in the silence, the Old World's magic awakens.

In places, not so special, in homes not so grand,
creatures of the Old World still peek out from their
sleeping holes and venture out into the world's deep
night.

From the ancient time of Vikings and legend, the Magic of the Old World exists. Runes and stories, myths and tales all live in our world today. Magical creatures hidden from sight still watch through mists and shadow.

The little being that comes out now is not like those scary things that wrestle in the deepest pit of night. He is not like the Night Mares, who trample into our minds with bad dreams and restless sleep.

He is not like the trolls of the bridges and stone, who
would grind our bones for soup and bread.

He is known by many names in many places. In
Norway, he is called Nisse. Other Scandinavian
countries have called him Tomte, Tonttu, Tomtenisse.
He is a gentle being of the Old World.

Dressed in a red cap, he has the kindly face of a little old man. His sparkly black eyes are for seeing in the dark. Small in stature, he bears pointed ears, only four fingers on each hand, and a fluffy white beard.

This little Nisse, aged and wise as the land he lives on, is quiet and unseen for he is a shapeshifter, taking the form of any of the animals he calls friend.

Long has he been of the land, long has he watched over the house and the people. He is a friend to all who mean the world no harm.

No one sees the Nisse.
He watches over us quietly, hiding when we are around, changing to his animal forms, sneaking silently. If you are very lucky, in the morning after a night of fresh fallen snow, you can see his tiny footprints in the drifts.

There are times, if you are very still, you may hear the whispered songs and poems of his ancient language, telling tales to himself and his animal friends. On cold nights, he might be heard using his willow flute, soothing quiet music into the night.

He watches over the animals of the household. So, keep your pets healthy, clean, and safe from harm. Be kind to the creatures of the world, or the Nisse will be angered.

Often, with a companion like an old cat or curious fox, sometimes an owl, he patrols the grounds, keeping bad spirits and nightmares away.

During the winter celebrations, Nisse were said to bring gifts, begetting joy and cheer to last throughout the year.

In olden times, families left out porridge. It is very important not to forget the little pad of butter atop the food, for what is porridge without the delicious golden tab of butter the Nisse love so much?

Some say the Nisse are no longer around, gone like so many of the mythical creatures of the Old World. Today, they say all that remains are the memories of the little man, remembered with pictures, tales, decorations, and figures.

But we know the Nisse is a cunning little shapeshifter. Is Old Magic ever truly gone from the world? So, remember the helpful, vigilant little Nisse. He is a spirit of the Norse folklore, a creature of its northern legends. There could be one watching over your own home.

The Art of Rosemaling

Rosemåling, or rosemaling, is a Scandinavian decorative folk art painting, originating in parts of Norway. Rosemåling is usually painted on wood and uses stylized flowers, scrollwork, lines, and other stylized elements.

Rosemaling came into existence in 1750, in the rural areas of Norway, and was used to cover ceilings, walls, furniture, wooden bowls, boxes, and trunks. Typically, Rosemaling was done by farmers as an additional source of income and was most common by farmers with smaller farmsteads.

By the 1900's, Rosemaling had gone out of style, but in the 1940, the work of Per Lysne, an immigrant who moved to Stoughton, Wisconsin, began a surge of popularity of Rosemaling in the United States. Since then, the interest in Rosemaling has increased and can be found being taught throughout the United States.

The artwork seen in this book has been created using digital painting in the Rosemaling style, utilizing digital canvas and brush to bring the traditional technique to the new modern medium.

The Nisse of Scandinavia

A Nisse is a mischievous domestic sprite, which cares for and protects a specific farmstead or home dwelling. This mythological creature from Scandinavian folklore is often associated with the Christmas season and is considered the Swedish and Norwegian version of Santa Claus.

In ancient times, they were believed to be the soul of the first homesteader of the land. Most commonly described as an older man, small in size, with a beard and red cap. He is considered a house guardian as long as he is respected and trusted by the owners or residents of the household.

In the 1800's, Nisse became the bearer of Christmas presents throughout Scandinavia. Some depictions now appear a bit more like the American Santa Claus, but within the Scandinavian countries, his traditions are still rooted in local culture. He lives in a forest nearby as opposed to the North Pole. His reindeer, sometimes goats, do not fly but assist in pulling his sleigh.

Garden gnomes are thought to be a representation of the Nisse. Garden gnomes can be placed into a yard to bless it with good fortune, much like a Nisse was a blessing to a home.

In modern Norway, Nisse are often seen as beardless, but always with the trademark red cap. They are often pictured watching over a home or keeping eyes on the children of the home.

Kari L. Ronning
Author and Artist

Kari is the principle artist and author of the publishing company, Three Muses Ink. She is a full time artist and writer with a Bachelor's of Art from the University of Alaska. Kari is an award-winning photographer who specializes in digital composites, digital and traditional drawing and painting, and graphic design.

Passionate about writing and storytelling, she's been a spinner of tales and an imaginative illustrator since grade school. A long-standing love of elves, myth, and legends influenced by her Norwegian and Chinese heritage, sparked a talent in creating fantasy themed novels, art and narratives. Across multiple genres, the interests have come together in works such as the Haunted Weir Workings series, Nisse at Night, a fully illustrated Norwegian themed children's story, and many other projects from Three Muses Ink.

Three Muses Ink

Three Muses Ink is a trio of authors and artists from the great northern state of Alaska. Always fans of fantasy and storytelling, the love affair with the idea of creating our own world started early. We are inseparable friends who have turned our passion into an independent publishing company, Three Muses Ink, producing novels, storybooks, artwork, and all manner of artistic creations.

To find out more about Three Muses Ink projects check out our website:
www.3MusesInk.com

www.3MusesInk.com

www.ingramcontent.com/pod-product-compliance
Lightning Source LLC
Chambersburg PA
CBHW041031170626
46815CB00001B/52